Ladybird books are widely available, but in case of
difficulty may be ordered by post or telephone from:

Ladybird Books – Cash Sales Department
Littlegate Road Paignton Devon TQ3 3BE
Telephone 0803 554761

A catalogue record for this book is available
from the British Library

Published by Ladybird Books Ltd Loughborough Leicestershire UK

THE TALE OF
PETER RABBIT™

Based on the original and authorized story
by Beatrix Potter
Ladybird Books in association with Frederick Warne

Once upon a time there were four little rabbits. Their names were Flopsy, Mopsy, Cotton-tail and Peter. They lived in a sandbank underneath the root of a very big fir-tree.

One morning they were allowed to play outside.

"Don't go into Mr McGregor's garden," their mother warned. "Your father had an accident there. He was put in a pie by Mrs McGregor.

"Now run along and don't get into mischief," said Mrs Rabbit. "I am going out."

Then she took her basket and umbrella and set off for the baker's. She wanted to buy a loaf of bread and some currant buns.

Now Flopsy, Mopsy and Cotton-tail
were good little rabbits. They went
down the lane to pick blackberries.
But Peter was naughty.
He ran straight away to
Mr McGregor's garden.

There were lots of vegetables in Mr McGregor's garden. Peter began to eat them. First he ate some lettuces and some French beans. Then he ate some radishes.

Soon, Peter had eaten too much. Feeling sick, he went to look for some parsley. "That will make me feel better," he said to himself.

But whom should he meet but
Mr McGregor!

Mr McGregor jumped up
and ran after
Peter, waving
a rake.

"Stop thief!" he
shouted angrily.

Peter was very frightened and rushed
away as fast as he could. As he was
running through the cabbage patch
he lost one of his shoes. Then he lost
the other shoe amongst the potatoes.

Peter started to run on all four legs and went much faster, but he had forgotten the way back to the gate. Unfortunately he ran into a gooseberry net and got caught by the large brass buttons on his jacket.

Peter was trapped! He started to cry, but his sobs were overheard by some sparrows who flew over to him.

"Keep trying!" they chirped. "Don't give in!"

So Peter stopped crying and tried to free himself. Then, as Mr McGregor came up with a sieve to pop over Peter's head, he wriggled out just in time!

Peter ran towards the tool-shed, leaving his little blue jacket behind him. When he got inside, he jumped into a watering can.

Mr McGregor was quite sure that Peter was hiding in the tool-shed and began to look for him underneath the flower-pots.

Mr McGregor couldn't find Peter anywhere. But the watering can had water in it and soon Peter started to sneeze.

"*Kertyschoo*!"

Mr McGregor was after him in no time.

Peter jumped out of a window before Mr McGregor could catch him. The window was too small for Mr McGregor and he was tired of running after Peter.

He went back to his work.

Peter sat down to rest. After a time he began to wander about, going lippity, lippity – not very fast, and looking all around. He found a door in the wall, but it was locked. Then he met a mouse and asked her the way to the gate. But she had a large pea in her mouth and couldn't answer.

Presently Peter came to a pond.

A white cat was sitting very, very still, staring at some fish. Peter thought it best to go away without speaking to her. He had heard about cats from his cousin, Benjamin Bunny.

Peter went back towards the tool-shed,
but suddenly, quite close to him,
he heard the noise of a hoe –
scr-r-ritch, scratch, scratch, scritch.

Peter climbed up onto a wheelbarrow
and peeped over. The first thing he
saw was Mr McGregor hoeing onions.
His back was turned towards Peter,
and beyond him was the gate!

Peter climbed down very quietly from the wheelbarrow and started running. Mr McGregor caught sight of him but Peter did not care. He slipped underneath the gate and was safe at last in the wood outside the garden.

Back in the garden Mr McGregor
hung up the little blue jacket and
shoes as a scarecrow.

Peter never stopped running or
looked behind him till he got home
to the big fir-tree. He was so tired
that he flopped down onto the sandy
floor and shut his eyes.

Mrs Rabbit was busy cooking. She noticed that Peter's jacket and shoes were missing. It was the second little jacket and pair of shoes that Peter had lost in a fortnight!

Peter was not very well during the evening. His mother put him to bed and made some camomile tea.
She gave a dose of it to Peter.

"One tablespoon to be taken at bedtime," she said.

But Flopsy, Mopsy and Cotton-tail
had bread and milk and blackberries
for supper.